This Ladybird Book belongs to:

This Ladybird retelling
by
Audrey Daly

Ladybird books are widely available, but in case of
difficulty may be ordered by post or telephone from:

Ladybird Books – Cash Sales Department
Littlegate Road Paignton Devon TQ3 3BE
Telephone 0803 554761

A catalogue record for this book is available
from the British Library

Published by Ladybird Books Ltd Loughborough Leicestershire UK
Ladybird Books Inc Auburn Maine 04210 USA

Hansel
and Gretel

illustrated
by
PETER STEVENSON

based on the story by Jacob and Wilhelm Grimm

Once upon a time, a boy called Hansel and his sister Gretel lived with their father and stepmother in a cottage near a forest.

They were so poor that they sometimes did not have enough to eat. One day the children heard their stepmother say to their father, "Tomorrow we must take the children deep into the forest and leave them there. Otherwise *we* shall starve."

Gretel was frightened, but Hansel had a plan. That night, when everyone was asleep, he crept outside and filled his pockets with shiny white pebbles.

The next morning, when the family went into the forest, Hansel walked more slowly than the others. When no one was looking, he dropped his pebbles along the path.

As soon as they were deep in the forest, their stepmother left the children by themselves, telling them to wait until someone came to fetch them. They waited until it grew dark, but no one came.

At last the moon rose. Hansel showed Gretel the pebbles he had dropped. They shone white in the moonlight and showed the children the way home.

When the tired, hungry children
arrived back at the cottage, their
father was very glad to see them.

But their stepmother was angry.
Next day she told the woodcutter
that they would have to take the
children into the forest again.

"And this time we must see that they *can't* find their way home!"

That night, when everyone was asleep, Hansel got up to collect some pebbles again. But his stepmother had locked the door and hidden the key. Hansel could not get out.

In the morning, before they all
set off, their stepmother gave
the two children a small piece
of bread each for their lunch.

They hadn't gone very far before
Hansel began to walk more slowly
than the others.

"Why are you so slow?" his
stepmother shouted, looking
back at him. "Hurry up!"

"I'm only saying goodbye to my
friends the birds," said Hansel.
But he was really stopping to drop
breadcrumbs along the path.

When they had gone deep into the forest, the woodcutter lit a small fire for his children. Sadly, he told them to wait beside it until someone came to fetch them.

The children waited until it grew dark, but no one came.

When the moon rose, Hansel and Gretel looked for the trail of breadcrumbs to lead them home.

But there wasn't a single crumb to be seen. The birds had eaten them all!

The children tried to find their way out of the forest, but they didn't know which path to take. They were completely lost.

Hansel and Gretel were tired and frightened and very, very hungry. They had no idea where to go or what to do next.

Suddenly Gretel cried, "Hansel, look!" Just ahead of them was a strange little house made of cakes and gingerbread, with a roof of sugary icing.

Laughing with pleasure, the children broke off bits of the house and began to eat.

Suddenly the door of the little house creaked open. An old woman looked out.

"Hello, children," she said, smiling. "Come inside, and I will give you food and somewhere warm to sleep."

The children went into the house, and she gave them some delicious pancakes and milk. In the back room there were two little beds.

Hansel and Gretel were happy to be safe at last with such a kind woman. They didn't know that she was really a wicked witch who liked to eat little children!

Next day the witch put Gretel to work scrubbing the floors. Then she took poor Hansel and locked him in a cage. "I'm going to fatten you up and eat you!" she cackled. "I'm looking forward to that!"

Every morning the witch, who had very poor eyesight, told Hansel to hold out his finger so that she could feel how fat he had grown.

But each time clever Hansel held out a chicken bone instead.

"Not nearly fat enough yet," the witch would mutter.

Days went by, and Hansel kept holding out a chicken bone instead of his finger.

At last the witch grew impatient. "I'm not waiting any longer! He *must* be fat enough by now," she said one morning. "Today I'm going to cook Hansel and eat him. Gretel, light the oven."

With tears in her eyes, Gretel did as she was told.

"Now, climb in and see if the oven is hot," the witch ordered.

But Gretel was sure that the witch was trying to trick her. "I can't climb into the oven," she said. "I'm much too big."

"Of course you can," said the witch angrily. "Look, I'll show you." And she bent down and stuck her head in the oven.

Gretel didn't waste a second. She gave the witch a hard push and slammed the door. The witch screamed with rage, but she couldn't get out.

When Gretel was sure the witch was dead, she unlocked Hansel's cage and let her brother out.

"We're free!" she cried. "We can go home now!"

But first Hansel and Gretel searched the witch's house from top to bottom. In the attic, they were amazed to find chests full of pearls and rubies and diamonds.

"We must take some of these home to Father," said Hansel.

As the children set off, Hansel
saw a white dove flying high
above. "It's one of my friends
showing us the way!" he said.

Soon the children saw their own cottage through the trees. Their father was overjoyed to see them.

"Your stepmother has gone, and she is never coming back," he said, hugging the children.

When he saw the jewels, the woodcutter couldn't believe his eyes. "We're rich!" he cried. "And we shall never be parted again."

And they never were.